Betty Rubble

Barney Rubble

Baby Puss

Bamm-Bamm

Fred Flintstone wants to make a new swimming pool, and he gets Barney to help him. But it's all too much like hard work, so they kidnap a brontosaurus to do the digging. And that's when the trouble starts...

British Library Cataloguing in Publication Data
Grant, John, *1930-*
    The Brontonappers.
    I. Title   II. Davies, Robin, *1950-*
823'.914 [J]
    ISBN 0-7214-1220-3

First edition

Published by Ladybird Books Ltd Loughborough Leicestershire UK
Ladybird Books Inc Auburn Maine 04210 USA

Printed in England

THE FLINTSTONES

in
The Brontonappers

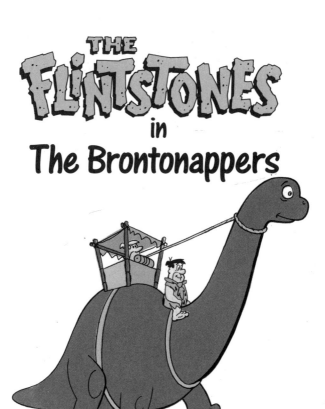

by JOHN GRANT
illustrated by ROBIN DAVIES

Ladybird Books

Wilma Flintstone was sitting drinking a cup of coffee in her kitchen when her friend Betty Rubble dropped in.

"I'm ashamed of this kitchen," said Wilma. "The cupboard doors are falling off. The pipes leak. The oven won't heat. And the fridge refuses to freeze."

"Can't you get Fred to fix everything?" asked Betty. "He and Barney have a holiday next week for Bedrock Founders' Day. Barney certainly isn't doing anything."

"Good idea," said Wilma.

But Fred had other ideas. While the girls drank their coffee, he and Barney were in the backyard where Fred had marked a large square shape on the ground.

"Barney," said Fred, "I am about to achieve the ambition of a lifetime."

"Pay back all the money you owe?" said Barney.

Fred ignored that. "I'm going to have my own swimming pool," he said. "Right here."

"Swimming pools are very expensive, Fred," said Barney. "You need pumps and filters and things."

"Mere extras!" said Fred. "A swimming pool is a hole in the ground with water in it. It won't cost us a penny."

"Us?" said Barney.

"You don't think I'd leave my old pal out of a great scheme like this?" said Fred. "Just be here sharp on Bedrock Founders' Day holiday. And bring a spade."

Digging the hole for the swimming pool was easier said than done. By the middle of the day it was only knee-deep. The ground was all rocks. Fred and Barney puffed and panted as they heaved the rocks out of the hole.

"Some holiday this is," said Fred. "I might as well be at my job in Slate's Stone Quarry.

At least I get paid for working there. And I have a brontosaurus to do the hard work. Wait a minute!"

"Thanks, Fred," said Barney. "I could do with a rest."

"That's given me an idea," said Fred. "We'll borrow a bronto from the quarry. "

"Will Mr Slate lend you one?" asked Barney.

"We'll just borrow one," said Fred. "We don't need to ask."

As soon as it was dark, Fred and Barney set out for the quarry.

"Isn't there a watchman?" asked Barney, nervously.

They could hear loud snores, and Fred pointed to a wooden office. The watchman was asleep. Barney climbed up and unfastened the gate of the brontosaurus pen. Fred swung the gate open. He whistled softly. "Here, boy," he called. "That's a good bronto."

One of the huge animals followed him out of the pen, and Barney closed the gate.

Bedrock was asleep as they rode the brontosaurus to Fred's house. The moon shone brightly as the big animal started shifting the rocks. Then it stopped and lay down!

"Perhaps it's hungry," said Barney.

Fred brought out a load of groceries from the kitchen. The brontosaurus looked at the heap of fruit, vegetables, loaves of bread, cans of soup and bottles of milk… and swallowed the lot in one gulp. Then it got to its feet and started work again.

The hole was getting deep by the time it lay down the second time. More food got it working again. But after the sixth time Fred said, "There's no food left."

"There's one chocolate chip cookie," said Barney, holding it up.

The brontosaurus snapped the cookie from Barney's hand. Then it stuck its head through the kitchen window and began to hunt for something more to eat.

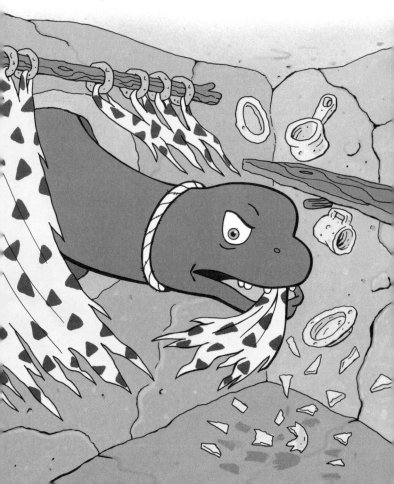

There was a scream from inside Fred's house as Wilma woke to find a brontosaurus with its head through the window, wrecking the kitchen. It backed out quickly as she banged it on the nose with a rolling pin. Its huge tail swung round... and swept all the rocks back into the hole!

"Now look what you've done!" shouted Fred. "We'll have to start all over again!"

"You'll start nothing!" cried Wilma, rushing out of the house still waving her rolling pin. "You'll take this thing back where you found it! Right now!"

But the brontosaurus had caught sight of the rolling pin, and was already squeezing its way out through the gate.

Then – it lay down in the road!

Barney quickly dashed over to his own house. In a moment he was back with Betty, each carrying armloads of food.

The brontosaurus gulped it down, but it still didn't get up. It wasn't until Betty said, "There's not a crumb left. I don't know what we're going to do for breakfast!" that the huge animal slowly got to its feet.

"Come on, Barney," said Fred. "Let's take him home."

At the mention of home the brontosaurus perked up.

Fred and Barney climbed onto its back and headed it in the direction of Slate's Stone Quarry.

Wilma and Betty watched until the brontosaurus with Fred and Barney disappeared in the darkness.

"I'd ask you in for a cup of coffee, Betty," said Wilma. "My kitchen was a mess before… now it's a total ruin!"

"Come over to my place," said Betty.

As they drank their coffee in the Rubbles' living room, Betty said, "Let's have some music," and switched on the radio. She had barely tuned into a late-night pop programme when the music was interrupted.

"Here is a police message," said the announcer. "A brontosaurus has been reported kidnapped from Slate's Stone Quarry. Mr Slate has personally offered a handsome reward for its return."

"Fred and Barney will go to jail if they're caught!" cried Betty.

"If the judge gives them hard labour," said Wilma, "I'll suggest that they do it rebuilding my kitchen!"

Meanwhile, the brontosaurus was plodding its way through the sleeping streets of Bedrock. Barney peered about him. "Hey, Fred, do you know where we are? We should have reached the quarry ages ago."

"Eh?" said Fred. "I must have dozed off. I can hardly keep my eyes open. It's been a very busy night."

"*This* looks like the right road," said Barney. There was no reply from Fred. He had fallen asleep again.

A moment later, so had Barney.

It had been a busy night for the brontosaurus as well as Fred and Barney. It began to feel sleepy. A short nap would do very nicely. It began to fold up its legs and stretch its neck out along the ground.

Fred woke with a start to find himself sliding down the brontosaurus' neck. With a yell he somersaulted over its head and in through an open door. Looking down at him was a very surprised policeman. He was in the police station.

"Can I help you, sir?" asked the constable.

Another policeman shouted. "Hi! There's a brontosaurus out there. Is it yours, sir?"

Barney came in. "No, it's not his," he said. "We were bringing it from his backyard to…"

But the first policeman was already shouting into the telephone.

"Mr Slate! We've got your brontosaurus. It seems it turned up in some fellow's backyard!"

Mr Slate arrived at the police station.

"Good heavens!" he cried. "Flintstone!"

"It seems," said the policeman, "that whoever kidnapped your brontosaurus abandoned it on Mr Flintstone's property. Mr Flintstone has fed it, and brought it in here. A very public-spirited citizen, if I may say so."

"You may, indeed," said Mr Slate. "Flintstone, of all people. Come to my office in the morning and I'll pay you the reward. Goodnight."

When he got home, Fred was so tired that he only just managed to tell Wilma of the reward for the missing brontosaurus before he fell asleep.

First thing in the morning he would phone the swimming pool company!

Fred slept late. He woke with Barney tapping on the bedroom window.

"Barney, old buddy," he cried. "Come in! Get the phone book while I dress. Look up Bedrock Swimming Pools Limited. Slate's reward money will buy the best pool in the world!"

"I think you should take a look outside first, Fred," said Barney.

Fred leaned out of the window. A truck was parked in front of the house. On the side was painted, BEDROCK KITCHEN COMPANY. And he could hear some very noisy hammering and banging.

"It only seems right," said Wilma as Fred looked in dismay at the men tearing out the old kitchen. "Mr Slate's brontosaurus wrecked my kitchen. His reward money will pay for the new one. Now hurry down to the office and collect it before he finds out what really happened… and changes his mind."